To Adrienne
Stuart Duncan

Alice Falls Apart

Written by Perry Nodelman
Illustrated by Stuart Duncan

Bain & Cox, Publishers
Winnipeg

Alice Falls Apart first published 1996 by
Bain & Cox, Publishers
an imprint of Blizzard Publishing Inc.
73 Furby Street, Winnipeg, Canada R3C 2A2

Printed in Canada by Friesens Printers.
Published with the assistance of the Canada Council
and the Manitoba Arts Council.

Canadian Cataloguing in Publication Data

Nodelman, Perry
Alice falls apart
ISBN 0-921368-65-8
I. Duncan, Stuart. II. Title.
PS8577.033A755 1996 jC813'.54 C96-920077-3
PZ7.N64A1 1996

For my daughter,
a different Alice altogether.
—Perry Nodelman

To Avelyn, who often falls apart,
and to Bronwen, who keeps us together.
—Stuart Duncan

It was suppertime.

"Today I had an argument with myself about buying some new shoes," said Momma.

"I'm glad you stopped yourself," said Poppa.

Momma noticed Alice playing with her spaghetti.

"Behave yourself, Alice," she said.

"Yes, Alice," said Poppa, "Control yourself. And," he added, "help yourself to the cheese."

MILK

When Alice woke up the next morning, she rolled over and bumped into somebody. The somebody looked just like Alice. The somebody was sound asleep.

When Alice shook the other Alice and asked her who she was, the other Alice said, "I'm Alice, of course. Go away. I'm sleeping. I love sleeping. I'm going to sleep all day."

But it was a school day, so Alice punched the sleepy Alice until she woke up, and then she made sure that the sleepy Alice got dressed almost as fast as she did herself.

At breakfast the sleepy Alice kept yawning and falling into the cereal bowl. Momma said, “Alice, watch your manners.” Alice watched the sleepy Alice’s manners, and decided they were crummy.

MILK

When they got outside there was another Alice climbing the crab apple tree. Alice told this new Alice that Poppa didn't let her climb that tree because it was too dangerous. The new Alice said, "So what?" She waved her arms and nearly fell.

Alice told the new Alice to cut it out. She ordered the new Alice to help her to get the sleepy Alice onto the bike. The new Alice made an ugly face, but she did what Alice said.

As soon as they were all on the bike, the sleepy Alice fell asleep again, and Alice had to hold her up. The new Alice tried riding with no hands, and nearly toppled the bike over.

SALE

At school, the three Alices had trouble squeezing into the desk. The sleepy one soon fell asleep. The nasty one made spitballs out of Alice's Language Arts homework and threw them at Mrs. Mackenzie. Whenever Alice tried to wake up the sleepy one, the nasty one would throw a spitball. Whenever Alice tried to stop

that one from throwing a spitball, the sleepy one would fall asleep again. Alice started to get mad.

One of the spitballs hit Mrs. Mackenzie, and Mrs. Mackenzie yelled at the Alices.

"You'll have to control yourself, Alice," said Mrs. Mackenzie.

Alice got madder. She shrieked.

Another Alice suddenly showed up, and started shouting terrible names at Mrs. Mackenzie. Alice was so embarrassed she blushed. The nasty Alice just giggled.

THINK
about
BEANS

"Remove yourself from this room," Mrs. Mackenzie said. She sent them to the principal's office.

Alice had to carry the sleepy one. The angry one was so angry that she said more bad words to Mrs. Mackenzie and Alice had to drag her away. The nasty Alice hopped on Alice's back and yelled, "Giddy-up, horsie!"

ON 6
108
BAS
SUMMER
Fun!!

When the principal asked why they'd been sent to see her, another Alice showed up. This Alice was so nervous that she shivered and shook and fainted dead away. The angry Alice thought about how unfair Mrs. Mackenzie was and got

even angrier. The nasty Alice snapped her gum and made a rude noise. The sleepy Alice slept.

The principal took one look at them all and sent them home for the day. “Get yourself together by tomorrow, Alice,” she said.

By the time they got home there were fourteen Alices. Some were carrying others who were asleep or unconscious. Some played. Some thought. Some screamed. Two of them argued with each other about whether they should buy some more gum or save their allowances.

One kept saying, “Go away, go away, I want to be alone,” to another one, who kept saying, “Now, now, nice girls should always smile. Go ahead now, Alice, dear, smile.” One of them kept pinching the others in the bum and then running away and laughing.

They all tried to get through the front door at the same time. It made a lot of noise.

Poppa shouted from the kitchen. “Alice, Alice, Alice! What a racket! I had a hard day, and I have a headache. You need to get a grip on yourself, Alice! Right now, Alice!”

As soon as they heard Poppa yell at them, the Alices immediately stopped fighting. They all turned to each other, and all at the same time, they all said, “Humph! Just who does he think *he* is, anyway? He’s not my boss, even if he is my father. And even if I love him, sometimes. What a loudmouth! What a dummy!”

Just one Alice walked into the kitchen, smiled sweetly at Poppa, and said “Boy, am I glad to see you!”

She gave him a kiss, sat down, and had a glass of milk and a cookie.

When Poppa asked her if she had a good day, Alice said, “No. Everything went wrong today, and I went to pieces. I completely fell apart. But you know, Poppa, I felt better as soon as I got control of myself.”

Poppa said, “Great, sweetie. How did you do it?”

Alice gave him a strange look and said, “Oh, I just did.”

MILK
MILK
SUDS

"That's easy for you to say, smartypants," said the hungry Alice, who showed up just long enough to take one more cookie that Alice didn't really want.

So of course Poppa said, “Enough, Alice, you’ll ruin your dinner.”
And then another Poppa showed up and said to Poppa, “Button your lip, fatface, and stop picking on the kid just because *we* have a headache.”

So he did button his lip, and he gave Alice a hug, and Alice hugged him back, and they both had another cookie.

Perry Nodelman has spent most of his adult life reading, enjoying and studying books for children and young adults. His first novel, *The Same Place But Different*, was published in 1993. Since then, Perry has written a sequel, many picture books, and co-authored *Of Two Minds* (Bain & Cox, 1994) with his friend Carol Matas. He lives in Winnipeg with his wife, their three children, and two miniature dachshunds.

As a child, **Stuart Duncan** was always drawing, deriving inspiration from his artistic father and the natural world around him. He has co-owned an art gallery with his wife, and has worked as an illustrator for an educational publisher. Stuart now works as a freelance illustrator in Victoria, B.C., where he lives with his wife and daughter.